Clifford
and the Dinosaurs

For Dashiell Winslow del Barco

The author would like to thank Frank Rocco and Grace Maccarone
for their contributions to this book.

Copyright © 2011 by Norman Bridwell.

Library of Congress Cataloging-in-Publication Data
Bridwell, Norman.
Clifford and the dinosaurs / by Norman Bridwell.
p. cm. -- (Scholastic reader. Level 1)
Summary: Although they look scary, Clifford the big red dog learns
that dinosaurs in a museum are not real.
ISBN 978-0-545-23143-5 (pbk.)
[1. Dogs--Fiction. 2. Size--Fiction. 3. Dinosaurs--Fiction. 4.
Museums--Fiction.] I. Title. II. Series.

PZ7.B7633Chk 2011
[E]--dc22

2010012775

ISBN 978-0-545-23143-5

10 9 8 7 6 5 4 3 2   11 12 13 14 15/0

Printed in the U.S.A. 40
First printing, September 2011

Clifford
and the Dinosaurs

Norman Bridwell

Cartwheel
·B·O·O·K·S·®

SCHOLASTIC INC.
New York   Toronto   London   Auckland
Sydney   Mexico City   New Delhi   Hong Kong

Emily and her friends are going
to Dino World today.

Do they go by car?

No. This is how they go.

Some birds are surprised
to see girls and boys up so high.

Some people are, too.

The girls and boys are happy
when they get to Dino World.

Clifford has never been here before.

He thinks the first dinosaur is real.
He gets scared.

But Clifford is brave.

He sniffs the dinosaur.

Then he tries to play with it.

Oops!

Clifford can see the dinosaur is fake.

Clifford and the children see
a very big dinosaur.

Then they see a very small dinosaur.

They see baby dinosaurs.
And they see dinosaur eggs.

They see a dinosaur with plates.

And they see a dinosaur with wings.

A little boy points to Clifford.
"What kind of dinosaur is that?"
he asks his mother.

"That's not a dinosaur," she says.

"That is a very big red dog."

"Is he real?" says the boy.

"No," says his mother.

Clifford wants to show her he is real.

She doesn't seem to like that.

Clifford and the children see
a dinosaur with very big teeth.
It is scary.

Just then, they hear a cry for help.

It is the mother of the little boy.
"My boy is lost!" she cries.

Clifford sniffs the mother.

Then he sniffs the air.

And he runs.
Everyone runs after him.

Clifford stops when he gets
to the dinosaur eggs.

Everyone else gets there, too.

The boy is happy to see Clifford.
The mother is happy to see the boy.

And Clifford is happy to help!

For Every
Individual...

Renew by Phone
269-5222

Renew on the Web
www.imcpl.org

For General Library Infomation
please call 275-4100